The One That Got Away

Got Away

by

Stephanie Baudet

Illustrated by Derry Dillon

First published July 01 in Great Britain by

Educational Printing Services Ltd.
Albion Mill, Water Street, Great Harwood, Blackburn BB6 7QR
Telephone (01254) 882080   Fax (01254) 882010
e-mail:enquiries@eprint.co.uk   web site:www.eprint.co.uk

ISBN 1-900818-87-6

Contents

Chapter 1

Petcare

'I've just had an idea,' said Mike. 'We want something to do in the holidays, right?'

'Right,' said Jon, still staring at the computer screen.

'Dad says he'll take us to the Wildlife Park. But we need some money to spend.'

'So?' Jon clicked the mouse a few times and Mike sighed with exasperation.

'Listen!' he said, sharply.

Both Jon and Mike's sister, Sophie, looked up.

'Mrs Sarbutt just came in and says she's going to visit her sister for a few days and would Mum look after her prize dahlias. She has a budgie and there's nowhere to leave him, so I said we'd look after him for her. It made me think. Lots of people have pets that need looking after while they're away.'

'There are plenty of kennels and catteries,' said Sophie.

'I know, but they only take dogs and cats.

Why don't we look after other things? Birds, rabbits, small animals like that! They could all stay in the old stable. They will
be easier to look after and keep clean in there.'

'You mean we charge for looking after them?' asked Jon, looking slightly more interested.

'Of course. The owners can bring their cages and enough food and pay a small amount for us to take care of them.'

'Like what?'

'Well . . . . it depends.'

'Get a piece of paper and we'll write it down,' said Jon, closing down the computer.

Soon they had a list drawn up.

Rabbits, guinea pigs and hamsters	-	£1 per week.
Gerbils and mice	-	75p per week.
Birds	-	50p per week.

Then they made out a notice to put in the paper shop window. It cost thirty pence for a week.

They swept out the stable and tidied it up ready for their guests.

It wasn't long before the first one arrived. That very afternoon, in fact. It was Sammy, a big white rabbit. Sophie squealed with delight.

The owner was a girl in Mike's class.

Her dad carried the hutch down to the stable while she told them about the cleaning and feeding of Sammy.

Jon wrote it down in an old exercise book

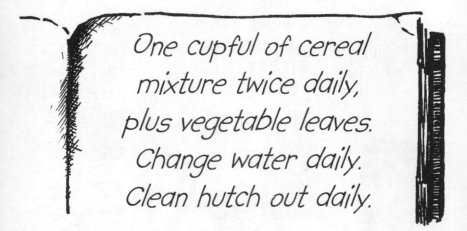

One cupful of cereal mixture twice daily, plus vegetable leaves. Change water daily. Clean hutch out daily.

Mike began to think that it was a lot of work for one pound a week.

Two gerbils came next, and two people came to book in a guinea pig, some stick insects and a canary for later in the holidays.

Jon wrote 'BOOKINGS' in the back of the exercise book and then filled in dates, names and type of animal.

'This is fun,' he said.

Mike beamed.

It was always difficult to know what to do when their cousin Jon came. He had to be prised away from the computer.

* * *

On Tuesday morning they went swimming. Mum had some shopping to do so she dropped them off at the pool for an hour and collected them later.

As they drove up to the house, they all stared . . . . Something was in the front garden.

'What is that?' asked Mum.

'It's a goat,' said Sophie.

'I can see that,' said Mum. 'But what's it doing here?'

Mike looked at Jon and they both giggled nervously. They hadn't quite got round to telling Mum and Dad about 'Petcare'.

'You're up to something,' said Mum, turning round in the driving seat and glaring at the two boys.

'It's our holiday job, Aunty Barbara,' explained Jon.

'Looking after small animals and birds while their owners are on holiday,' said Mike.

'Small animals?' said Mum, raising her eyebrows. 'So we won't be having any elephants or hippos then?'

All three of them giggled again.

'We put 'small' on the card,' said Mike.

Sophie was staring out at the goat. 'He's got a note tied to his rope,' she said.

'She,' said Mum. 'It's a nanny.'

Mum opened the gate and walked up to the goat which was tied to the trunk of a large shrub by a length of rope. All the leaves

on the lower branches had been eaten away
leaving only bare twigs.

'Oh dear,' said Mum, as she pulled off the
note while the goat butted her legs.

She quickly read the note to herself and
then read it out to the children:

Dear Petcare,

I am Hetty. You were out when I
came so I hope you don't mind me
waiting. My owner will be away
until Sunday. I'll keep your lawn cut
and you can drink my milk!
P.S. Please milk me twice a day.

Mum looked at the goat. 'Oh dear,' she said again.

'You won't have to buy milk this week,' said Mike, looking on the bright side. 'And Dad won't have to mow the lawn.'

'Take her round to the back,' said Mum, 'and find a stake to tie her rope to, otherwise she'll eat all our plants.'

* * *

Now, there was one disadvantage in having Hetty. The lawn was soon sprinkled with her small, currant-like droppings!

Several of these stuck to the soles of people's shoes and were brought into the house to be left, like tiny cowpats, on the kitchen floor.

Mum sighed. 'I can't have this,' she said, scraping them off the floor. 'You'll have to rake them up. I've got enough to do. I must go and water Mrs Sarbutt's dahlias. I'd hate to be responsible for her losing out to Mrs Howorth in the competition.'

Jon wasn't sure what to charge for Hetty. 'She is eating the grass and giving us milk,' he said. 'Even though she's not a small animal she's not much trouble.'

'Except for the droppings,' said Mike. 'We have to rake them up - and milk her.'

Jon sat down heavily on the bed.

'I think we should charge a pound - the same as for a rabbit.'

* * *

Later on there was a ring at the front door. As Mum was at Mrs Sarbutt's, watering her prize dahlias, Mike answered it.

A boy stood there holding a small box.

'We're going away tomorrow,' he said. 'Can you look after Wilberforce for me?'

'Yes,' said Mike, taking the box without asking what Wilberforce was.

'We'll be back on Sunday,' said the boy. 'Wilberforce eats crickets.'

Mike closed the door.

'Another pet,' he yelled up the stairs.

Jon and Sophie came running down, excitedly.

'What is it?' asked Sophie as she peered in through the glass panel at the front of the box.

Then she let out a long piercing shriek and ran back upstairs, tripping and stumbling as if she couldn't get up there fast enough.

Mike very nearly dropped the box but managed to put it down, safely, on the floor.

Then they both knelt down and bent to look inside.

A huge hairy black spider stood there

swaying slightly on its eight legs.

'Its a tarantula!' they gasped together.

Chapter 2

An Act of Goat

They both sprang to their feet. Then they stood as if frozen to the spot staring down at the small glass box.

'They're poisonous!' said Jon in a small voice.

'Deadly!' whispered Mike. 'What are we

going to do? I don't even know who the boy was. He's not coming back until Sunday.'

'We'll just feed it,' said Jon. 'Open the lid and pop the food in. It won't need cleaning out.'

'Spiders run fast,' said Mike, his voice shaking. 'Do you think we ought to tell Mum and Dad?'

Jon shrugged. 'We'd better take it to the stable.'

Neither moved.

'Go on, then,' said Jon. 'It was your idea.'

Mike stepped forward, warily, as if the spider might open the lid itself and jump out at him.

Slowly he reached down and picked up the box, every nerve in his fingers tingling.

He held the box out in front of him, never once looking at the spider and its eight long, hairy legs.

Sophie squealed from the top of the stairs making Mike jump and nearly drop it again.

Carefully, he carried the box through the kitchen and out of the back door, the other two following at a safe distance.

He knew if he dropped it the glass would break and . . .

At last he reached the stable, put the box down carefully on a shelf, and then they all ran back to the house. Sophie tripped over

Hetty's rope and sprawled on the grass.

'Uggh!' she said in disgust, looking at her hands. 'Mum said you had to rake up Hetty's droppings.'

'Me!' muttered Mike, irritably, 'you have to help too.'

Hetty was definitely not a loveable goat. She was stubborn and bad-tempered and tended to butt with one end and kick with the other.

* * *

Jon volunteered to milk her first. Mike held the goat's rope while Jon bent down at her side and put the bucket on the ground.

Then he grabbed one of her teats and squeezed. Only a few drops of milk came out and missed the bucket completely.

'That's not the way to do it,' said a voice.

They looked up to see Dad coming across the lawn. 'Haven't milked a goat since I was a lad,' he said, grinning. 'Here, let me have a go.'

He squatted down and repositioned the bucket under Hetty's udder.

'Now, you squeeze and pull at the same time, see? Like this.'

He took hold of one of Hetty's teats in each hand and squeezed and pulled the two teats alternately and two jets of milk spurted into the bucket.

'My, this takes me back,' he said, flinging his head back with a laugh.

Hetty chose that moment to rebel and kicked out with a hind leg. The flying hoof hit Dad's shoulder, taking him by surprise. He fell backwards onto the lawn, one foot shooting out and knocking over the bucket of milk.

All three laughed as Dad picked himself up.

'I don't like goat's milk much anyway,' he muttered, but finished the job anyway.

This time Hetty stood still.

None of them liked goat's milk.

'I thought it would taste the same as

ordinary milk,' said Mike, turning up his freckled nose.

'It's better for you,' said Mum. 'I'm going to use it in my Slimmer's cake for the W.I. fete.'

'Well, I think we ought to charge more than a pound for Hetty,' said Mike.

'Maybe one pound fifty,' agreed Jon.

* * *

The next morning there was some question as to whether they'd get any money at all.

Hetty was missing!

Mike had woken up early and looked out of his window, expecting to see the goat eating as usual.

But there was no Hetty.

There was one clue though. A hole in the hedge between their garden and Mrs Sarbutt's.

'Oh no!' groaned Mike, flinging back the bed clothes. He ran in to Jon's room and woke him. They both threw on some clothes and rushed outside.

One well-chewed end of Hetty's rope was still attached to the stake in the lawn.

The two boys squeezed through the hole in the hedge where she'd obviously eaten her way through.

And there she was, still eating. This time Mrs Sarbutt's prize dahlias!

It was getting beyond a joke!

Mike and Jon looked at each other in horror. Mrs Sarbutt would be furious! Beating Mrs Howorth at the W.I. fete on Saturday was very important to her.

'What are we going to do?' whispered Mike.

'You're the one with all the ideas,' said Jon, staring at the dahlia stalks. 'Rabbits and gerbils you said - and we end up with a horrible goat and a tarantula.'

They dragged the reluctant Hetty back through the hedge and tied her to the stake

with a double piece of rope. Then they tried
to pull the hedge together and patch up the
gap, as best they could, with twigs.

'Now, what about the dahlias?' asked Jon.

'We could say it was a natural disaster,'
said Mike.

'Like what?'

'Fire, flood, lightning - you know, they call
it an Act of God.'

Jon laughed. 'It was an act of goat!
That's not a natural disaster!'

* * *

It was Sophie who came up with an idea.

'We'll have to buy some more at the garden centre,' she said, 'and hope that Mrs Sarbutt doesn't notice.'

They went to the small garden centre at the back of a greengrocer's shop run by a Mr Cramhorn.

'What do you kids want?' he asked, suspiciously, as they walked up and down the rows of plants.

He was an oldish man, nearly bald and with a moustache that looked just like one of the bristly garden brooms standing in the corner. It was well-known that Mr Cramhorn did not like children.

'I'm watching you,' he said. 'You're up to no good. Kids have no interest in plants.'

'We'd like to buy a dahlia plant, please,' said Mike.

'Hm,' said Mr Cramhorn, looking as if he didn't quite believe them. 'What colour?'

The three looked at each other. What colour had they been? Hetty hadn't left much, except for a few petals.

'A sort of dark red,' said Mike, hoping desperately that he was right.
'Over here,' said Mr Cramhorn.

They followed him along another row of plants and there they were. A whole benchful of dahlias.

Mike chose the shade he thought was right and looked for the plant with the biggest flowers, knowing Mr Cramhorn was hovering over them all the time.

'I'll take this one, please.'

'Two pounds fifty,' said Mr Cramhorn, holding out his hand.

* * *

Mum was surprised when Mike and Jon offered to water Mrs Sarbutt's dahlias to save her the job.

'Water them well, but don't drown them,' she said.

They took the dahlia plant and a trowel from the garden shed. Then they went round into Mrs Sarbutt's garden.

Luckily, the soil was well dug and it didn't take them too long to dig up the old flowerless plant and put in the new one.

Mike pushed the soil down firmly round the plant as he'd often seen his dad do, then sat back on his heels.

'It's done,' he sighed, brushing the soil off his hands and feeling very proud of himself.

They both stood up, ready to go back, when suddenly Mrs Sarbutt's back door opened.

Mrs Sarbutt had come back from her sister's sooner than expected!

Chapter 3

Where is Wilberforce?

The two boys dived quickly behind the shed and then Mike peeped round the end.

With relief he saw Mrs Sarbutt stop at her dahlias, anxious to see if her prize flowers were all right.

She seemed to stare at them for a long

time and even bent down to get a closer look.

Then she stood up.

The two boys let out sighs of relief as the back door closed behind her.

* * *

On Saturday, Mike, Jon and Sophie were eating a late breakfast in the kitchen when Dad came in.

'You certainly spend a lot of time in the garden,' said Mum.

'Oh . . . er . . . well, the mower wanted cleaning,' said Dad.

Mike caught the sly glance he gave Mum.

What was Dad up to?

Come to think of it, both his parents had been acting a little strangely for some time.

Mum had made a New Year's Resolution and was on some sort of diet and hardly ate anything. She'd actually refused a chocolate the other day, and that was unheard of.

'I went to see those animals you're looking after,' went on Dad, grinning at the three children. 'Quite a collection, eh?'

'Speaking of animals,' said Mum, 'that awful goat has eaten one of your favourite blue socks that was hanging on the line.'

There was silence for a moment. Mike stole a look at his dad. He was beginning to wish he'd never thought of this idea. That goat was becoming a big problem!

Dad was frowning. 'I hope it's not staying too long,' he said. Then he looked at Mike. 'By the way,' he said, 'what was in that small box with the glass front? I found the lid wasn't on properly and whatever it was has escaped.'

Mike seemed to go cold all over. Jon nearly choked on his food and Sophie gave a squeal.

His idea had suddenly become a nightmare!

Dad was waiting for an answer and Mike tried to speak calmly, not looking him in the eye.

'Nothing too important, Dad. Just an insect.'

Mike tried not to think of the tarantula.

He thought of the W.I. fete that afternoon instead and that brought another pang of guilt . . . Mrs Sarbutt's dahlias.

But what should they do about the spider? There was no way any of them were going down to the stable to look for it.

A poisonous spider on the loose! They should tell Mum and Dad, even if they got into trouble. People's lives were at risk.

Should the police be called? And what would they do? Send out sniffer dogs? Mike didn't know.

Jon and Sophie got up from the table without speaking and put their dishes in the sink. Then they went upstairs. Cowards!

Dad went out too, leaving Mike alone with his mother.

'Mum . . . ' he began.

'Just a minute, Mike,' said Mum, putting some small cakes into a cake tin. 'I've got to get these ready for the fete. I'll just go and look for a box to put the tins in. I think there are some in the stable. Hang on a minute, I won't be long.'

She went out of the door and off across the lawn leaving Mike standing and staring after her through the window.

For two long minutes he watched, hardly

able to breathe, until at last she emerged from the stable, a big cardboard box in her hand.

'Now, what was it you wanted to say?' she asked, stacking the tins into the box.

'Er . . . about the pet that escaped . . .'

Mum paused briefly to look at him.

'Mike, I haven't time to listen to stories about your pets now,' she said, looking at her watch.

'Look at the time! You kids must be ready to go at twelve o'clock. You can buy a burger or something for your lunch when we get there.'

Mike went slowly upstairs. The other two were in Jon's room sitting on the bed.

'I tried to tell Mum,' said Mike, from the doorway. 'But she's too busy to listen.'

'Maybe it hasn't gone far,' said Sophie.

'We haven't looked.'

'Are you volunteering?' asked Mike.

Sophie said nothing.

'What we should have done,' said Jon,'was to get everyone's telephone number in case of emergencies. That's what boarding kennels do.'

'Well, we didn't, did we?' said Mike. 'It's

no help to say what we should have done.'

* * *

All three were silent in the car on the way to the fete.

'I'll be at the cake stall,' said Mum, getting out and opening the boot.

'After the competition we're going to sell the cakes. You three can wander round where you want.'

They watched her carry the box of cakes towards the marquee.

'What shall we do?' asked Jon.

Mike shrugged. He could always think of

better things to do than come to a W.I. Fete.

This time it was worse though. He had this big worry hanging over him.

'How about the dahlia competition?' suggested Sophie.

'Really exciting!' muttered Jon, but they all went to look for it anyway.

They found the place easily. It was actually in the same big marquee as the cake stall.

Mrs Sarbutt's loud voice could be heard above everyone else's as she hung over the table like a great vulture.

On the other hand, Mike thought, Mrs

Howorth could easily be compared to a mouse. Small, nervous and twitchy. She even had the odd whisker on her small pointed face.

Mrs Sarbutt was gloating over her blooms as if she'd already won first prize in the competition.

'But it's a funny thing,' she said, lowering her voice. 'They've changed colour - not much mind you, just a shade. Isn't that odd? Have you ever heard of anything like that happening before, Elsie?'

Mrs Howorth shook her head.

'Oh, here come the judges.'

Mrs Sarbutt smiled as the two men approached. 'Good afternoon, gentlemen,' she said, turning on the charm.

'It's Mr Cramhorn!' gasped Sophie.

He was, indeed, one of the judges.

As the competition began he carefully
studied all the entries, holding them up and
looking at the flowers from all angles,
measuring their size with a ruler.

However, when he got to Mrs Sarbutt's
plant he looked at it even more closely. His
eyebrows lowered into a frown and slowly
his thin mouth puckered up into a tight little
knot.

'Whose entry is this?' he thundered.

'Mine,' said Mrs Sarbutt in a puzzled

voice. 'Is something wrong?'

'Where did you get these flowers?'

'I grew them of course!' She shook with indignation.

'Madam,' said Mr Cramhorn, 'I recognise this particular shade. It's one of my own hybrids.'

Mrs Sarbutt was taken aback.

'Are you accusing me of cheating, Mr Cramhorn?' she shrieked.

At this point Jon grabbed Mike's arm.

'Let's get out of here quick before he recognises us!'

It wasn't difficult to slink away as quite a crowd was gathering at the sound of the raised voices.

* * *

At the other end of the marquee the cake competition was in full swing.

Mum's Slimmer cake (made with Hetty's milk) was the last to be judged.

One of the judges was looking at it now, bending over to study its texture, turning the plate this way and that and rubbing her chin from time to time as she did so.

Suddenly something caught Mike's eye.

Above the woman a loose end of rope hung from the roof of the marquee. And coming slowly down the rope, one hairy black leg after the other, was Wilberforce . . . the tarantula!

Chapter 4

Hairy Legs

When the spider got to the end of the rope it reached out another leg and waved it around in the air, searching for somewhere to put it.

The other seven legs moved down the rope until finally the spider could hold on no longer and it plopped gently down onto the

woman's back, its body bouncing up and down several times as it landed.

Everyone around the cake stall had seen it by now. It was too large a creature to miss.

Everyone held their breath and watched, fascinated, to see which way it would go next . . . Down her back and jump to the ground - or up into the forest of her hair.

A heavy silence hung over the little crowd, while not far away, Mrs Sarbutt and Mr Cramhorn still shouted at each other.

The woman judge was oblivious of the passenger she carried on her back and it seemed no-one was going to tell her.

'Very light and spongy,' she said, holding

the plate in the air and straightening up a
little. The spider almost lost its hold and the
crowd moved back with a gasp.

'Texture as delicate as a spider's web,'
she said. 'It certainly looks delicious.'

Mike suddenly had an urge to giggle
hysterically.

'I award this cake First Prize,' announced
the judge, straightening up suddenly and
taking Wilberforce by surprise so that he fell
off onto the ground.

With a shriek the crowd scattered
and then the woman looked down and saw
the tarantula. She didn't utter a sound
but fell forward in a faint - taking Mum's
prize-winning cake with her. Splodge! She

landed right on top of it.

Mike thought he'd never seen people move so quickly. Not even when the home-time bell went at school.

The woman judge lay on the ground, her face covered with cream (made with Hetty's milk) and her hair full of crumbs.

Under the cake stall table Mike had spotted the cardboard box Mum had brought the cakes in. The one that she'd fetched from the old stable. The spider must have been hiding in there all the time.

He shuddered! It was chaos!

Someone knocked into the trestle table and one end collapsed, all the cakes sliding down and landing in a heap on the ground.

These were then trampled in as people tried to get away, staring at the ground and trying to run without putting their feet down.

Children cried, women screamed and more stalls crashed to the ground.

Down at the plant stall the panic was catching. The large crowd there, which had gathered to watch the argument between Mrs Sarbutt and Mr Cramhorn, began running about without knowing why they were doing so.

Tables crashed down, water spilled, vases were smashed to pieces. Prize flowers which had received weeks of tender loving care were trampled and trodden underfoot in the stampede.

In the midst of all this, Mrs Sarbutt was finally silenced as she stared down at the carnage of red petals and broken leaves from her precious dahlias.

Mr Cramhorn suddenly yelled and started doing a strange dance, flinging his arms and legs into the air.

Mike, Jon and Sophie moved closer until they could see the reason for Mr Cramhorn's dance.

On his trouser leg, just above the knee, was Wilberforce, trying desperately to cling on.

Poor Wilberforce! He must be very frightened by all this, thought Mike. He must think there is an earthquake.

Then another thought struck him. If he was frightened - he might bite!

At last Mr Cramhorn did the only thing he could do. He took off his trousers.

The three children watched amazed, and Mike thought he must have easily broken the world speed record for taking off trousers.

One minute they were on, with Wilberforce clinging to the leg - and the next they were in a heap on the ground and Mr Cramhorn was off across the field in his underpants, his shirt flapping in the wind.

It was the funniest thing they'd ever seen.

For a moment they forgot about the

spider and their sides ached with laughter.

Then Mike reminded them that Mr
Cramhorn had to go all the way to the other
end of the High Street, and they shrieked
with laughter again.

* * *

Everyone had now gone. Everyone that is,
except for Mum, the lady judge, who was still
lying in a faint, the children and a tall man.

Mum looked very white and was staring at
the trousers on the ground.

'Is that . . . ?' she began.

'Yes, the insect that escaped from the
box,' finished Mike.

'I'm never going to be able to show my face at the Women's Institute again,' said Mum, weakly.

They were all silent for a moment, thinking of the terrible things that could happen because someone hadn't put the lid back properly on the box after feeding Wilberforce.

Then the man stepped forward.

'Excuse me,' he said, 'my name's Mr Earl and I'm an entomologist. I work at the Wildlife Park.'

He looked at the children. 'I look after the insects - and the spiders.'

He turned to Mum. 'Tarantulas are not

deadly, you know. Most people think they are but it's not true, otherwise they wouldn't be allowed as pets. They do bite, and it can be painful but not fatal.'

'Oh!' Mum let out a great sigh of relief. So did Mike and the others.

'What we must do now is catch him,' continued the man, bending down over the trousers.

'He's still in here I think, probably scared out of his wits. Can someone hand me one of those cake tins to put him in?'

Very carefully, he opened out the trousers and sure enough there was Wilberforce.

Mr Earl scooped the spider into his hand and popped him into the cake tin, shutting the lid firmly.

'You've done enough mischief for one day, my lad,' he said, as he handed the tin to Mike.

'Is it yours?'

'No, we're looking after it for someone while they're away on holiday.'

'I see,' said Mr Earl. 'Well, you'd better make sure he doesn't escape again. You can see what a panic it causes.'

He put a hand in his pocket and took three small pieces of paper from the bundle he had.

'If you'd like to come and see some more tarantulas as well as all my other creatures, here are some tickets for the Wildlife Park.'

Chapter 5

Guilty Secrets

Wilberforce's owner came for him the next day.

'Thanks,' he said, and paid his fifty pence. He grinned. 'Someone else in this town must have a tarantula. I heard that one was loose at the W.I. fete yesterday, did you know? Scared the pants off them too!' He giggled.

'Yeah?' said Mike, innocently.

He watched the boy go, carrying the small box. That spider wasn't so bad once you got used to it. He'd got to quite like it . . . well, a little bit.

Hetty's owner came too and they weren't sorry to see the back of the goat.

During the afternoon Mrs Sarbutt came round to collect her budgie and they all, including Mum and Dad, went to the stable to get him.

No-one mentioned the spider.

'There he is!' said Mrs Sarbutt rushing forward. Her foot caught a rake and she pitched forward, grabbing at an old cupboard to stop herself from falling.

A box of papers fell from the top and the door swung open. Inside were several boxes of chocolates.

'Aha!' said Dad. 'What's this? A secret hoard!'

Mum hung her head guiltily.

'So much for New Year's Resolutions,' said Dad.

'I did try,' said Mum. 'But sometimes I thought I'd die if I didn't have a chocolate.'

Sophie bent down to pick up one of the papers which had fallen on the floor.

'Whose are these?' she asked. 'They're all old Beano comics.'

'They're not mine,' said Mike, shaking his head.

Mum looked at Dad.

'Cleaning the mower?' she said. 'All that work in the garden?'

'Just a bit of light reading between jobs,' said Dad.

Mum looked at the three children. 'Well, none of us are perfect,' she said.

* * *

Mike had had another of his ideas.

'Oh no,' said Jon, holding his hands over his ears. 'I don't want to hear it.'

'Don't worry, said Mike, 'this one's got nothing to do with animals. You know it's Dad's birthday next week? Well, I've just thought what to buy him. That second hand bookshop is selling old Beano Annuals really cheap!'

Dad overheard what Mike said, and they all fell about, laughing.